Tabitha
and the
Raincloud

To Aaron and Jay, my dear, sweet
children: you are my silver lining
after every storm. And to those
who listen without judgement: for
so many, you are the guiding lights
which peak through the haze.
– D.S.

For Cody and Sam.
– M.J.

First published 2020

EK Books
an imprint of Exisle Publishing Pty Ltd
PO Box 864, Chatswood, NSW 2057, Australia
226 High Street, Dunedin, 9016, New Zealand
www.ekbooks.org

A CiP record for this book is available from the
National Library of Australia.

ISBN 978-1-925820-13-3

Designed by Mark Thacker
Typeset in Minya Nouvelle 16 on 23pt
Printed in China

This book uses paper sourced under ISO 14001
guidelines from well-managed forests and other
controlled sources.

10 9 8 7 6 5 4 3 2 1

Tabitha
and the
Raincloud

DEVON SILLETT & MELISSA JOHNS

EK

One morning, Tabitha woke up on the wrong
side of the bed. She soon discovered why.

'Hey! You're not supposed to be here,' she said.
'Go on! Scoot!'

But the raincloud wouldn't budge.

At breakfast, it rained all over her scrambled eggs.

'So soggy!' she moaned, spitting out a mouthful. 'Yuck!'

'You're welcome,' mumbled Dad under his breath.

During art, Tabitha tried very hard to concentrate
on her picture of a giraffe. But it was no use.

'What a lovely dinosaur,' complimented Ms Brushes.
Tabitha balled up her fists and growled up at the raincloud.

'This is all *your* fault!'

When it was library time, Tabitha stomped so hard on her way
to get her favourite book — all about how to do magic tricks — that she
tripped over with a *thud!*, and Angela McBurble got there first.

'Not fair!' cried Tabitha.

'It looks like you've already learned how to make everyone's smiles disappear,' muttered Angela.

At lunch, no one wanted to sit near Tabitha.
Not even her best friend Andy.

'Sorry,' said Andy, looking up at Tabitha's raincloud.
'You're just a bit too stormy today.'

'Go on then,' said Tabitha, scrunching up her nose. 'I was going to share some of my biscuits with you, but now I get them all to myself.' But she didn't really want them all to herself.

Then, Tabitha remembered something.

Suddenly, the raincloud wasn't so bad.

In fact, it was kind of fun. Really fun.

She sploshed and sloshed.
She rolled and dived.

She giggled so hard that she
fell right into her puddle.

But not even that could
dampen her mood!

One by one, the others came to join in the fun.

By the time lunch was over, Tabitha's raincloud had disappeared altogether.

That night, Tabitha made sure to bundle herself up in bed extra tight.

But, just in case she woke up next to a raincloud the next morning, she was ready.

by Tabitha